BLAST OFF TO EARTH!
A LOOK AT GEOGRAPHY

BLAST OFF TO EARTH!
A LOOK AT GEOGRAPHY

WRITTEN AND ILLUSTRATED BY

LOREEN LEEDY

HOLIDAY HOUSE NEW YORK

Library of Congress Cataloging-in-Publication Data

Leedy, Loreen.

    Blast-off to Earth! : a look at geography / Loreen Leedy. — 1st
ed.

       p.   cm.

    Summary: A group of aliens on a field trip visit each of the
continents on Earth and learn about some of their unique features.

    ISBN 0-8234-0973-2

    1. Geography—Juvenile literature.   [1. Geography.
2. Continents.]   I. Title.

G175.L44   1992   92-2567   CIP   AC
910—dc20

ISBN 0-8234-1409-4 (pbk.)

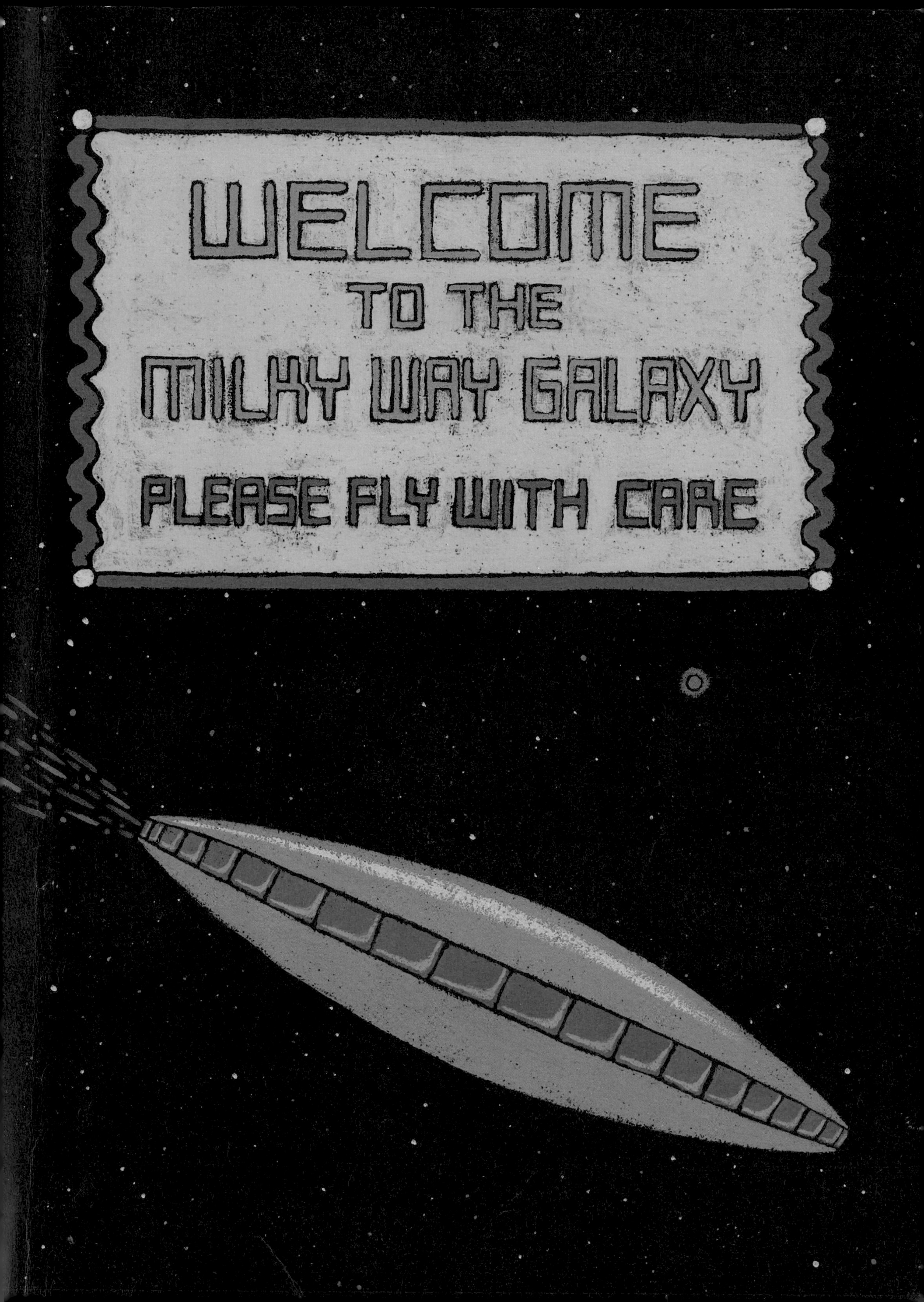
WELCOME
TO THE
MILKY WAY GALAXY
PLEASE FLY WITH CARE

How long till we get there, Mr. Quark?
Just a few more nanoseconds.
I have visual contact! It looks like a big, blue marble.
ROBOT WIRING

Soon we will see Earth up close.

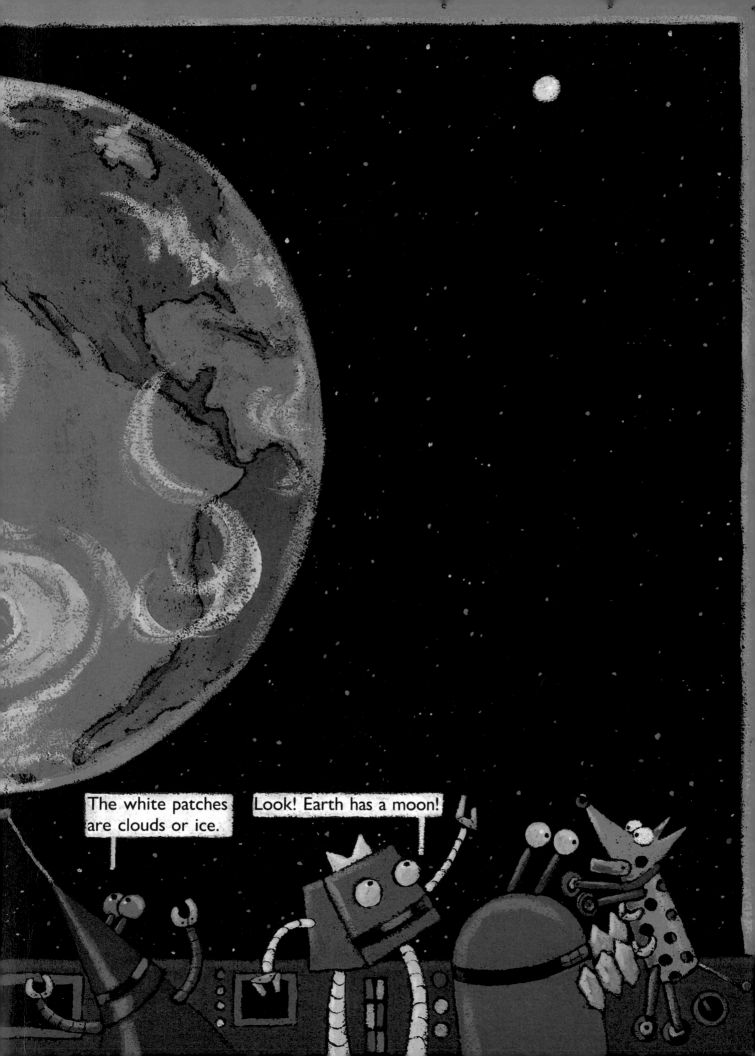

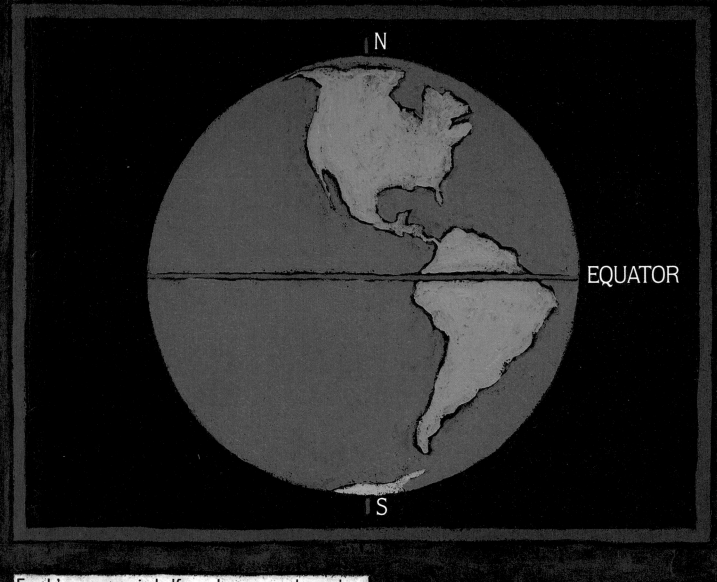

N

EQUATOR

S

Earth's equator is halfway between the poles.
The climate is hot near the equator.

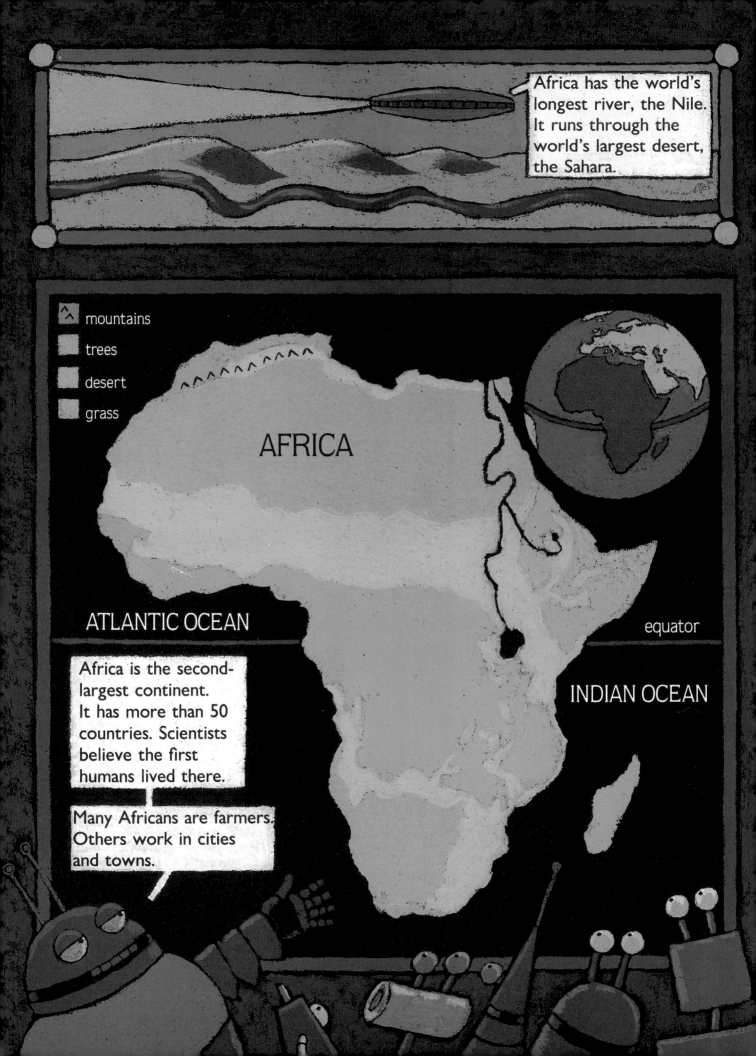

equator

Amazon River

SOUTH AMERICA

Brazil

PACIFIC OCEAN

Andes Mountains

ATLANTIC OCEAN

South America is the fourth-largest continent. It stretches from above the equator almost to the South Pole.

The Andes mountains run along the western edge of the land.

Most people speak Spanish. In the largest country, Brazil, people speak Portuguese.

mountains

trees

grass

desert

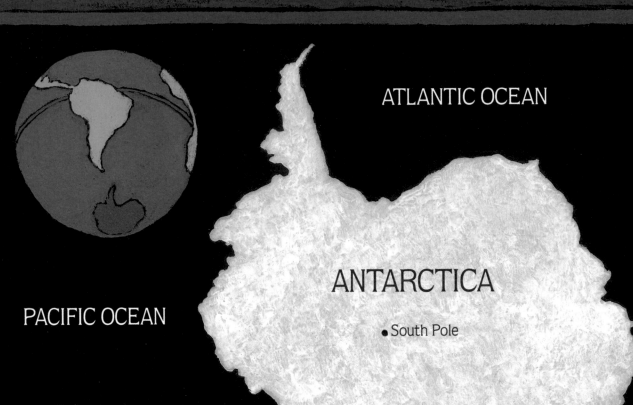

ATLANTIC OCEAN

ANTARCTICA

• South Pole

PACIFIC OCEAN

Antarctica is the fifth-largest continent. It is located at the South Pole, and is covered with ice. The ice is over a mile thick!

It is too cold for humans to live there.

INDIAN OCEAN

Just like scientists and explorers, we can visit Antarctica.

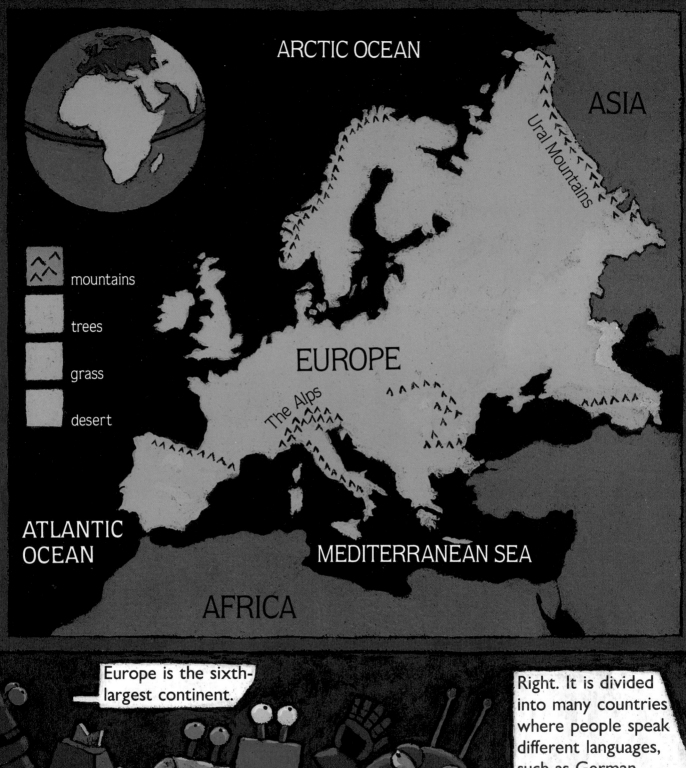

ARCTIC OCEAN

ASIA

Ural Mountains

EUROPE

The Alps

ATLANTIC
OCEAN

MEDITERRANEAN SEA

AFRICA

mountains

trees

grass

desert

Europe is the sixth-largest continent.

Right. It is divided into many countries where people speak different languages, such as German, French, and Polish.

Centuries ago, Europeans explored much of Earth's surface. Many humans left their homelands to live in other countries.

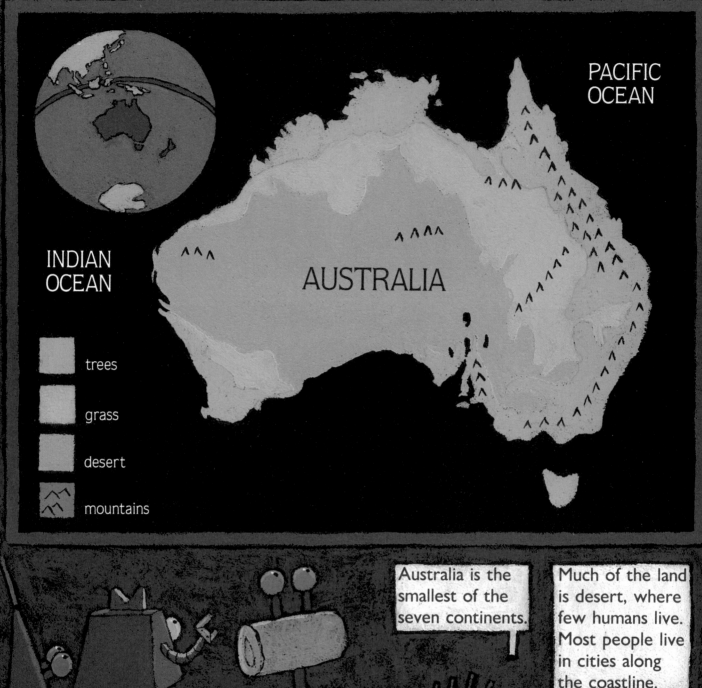

PACIFIC
OCEAN

INDIAN
OCEAN

AUSTRALIA

trees

grass

desert

mountains

Australia is the
smallest of the
seven continents.

Much of the land
is desert, where
few humans live.
Most people live
in cities along
the coastline.

All aboard! We are leaving Earth now!
Awwwww! Do we have to, Mr. Quark?
Yes. But we can come back again on another field trip.

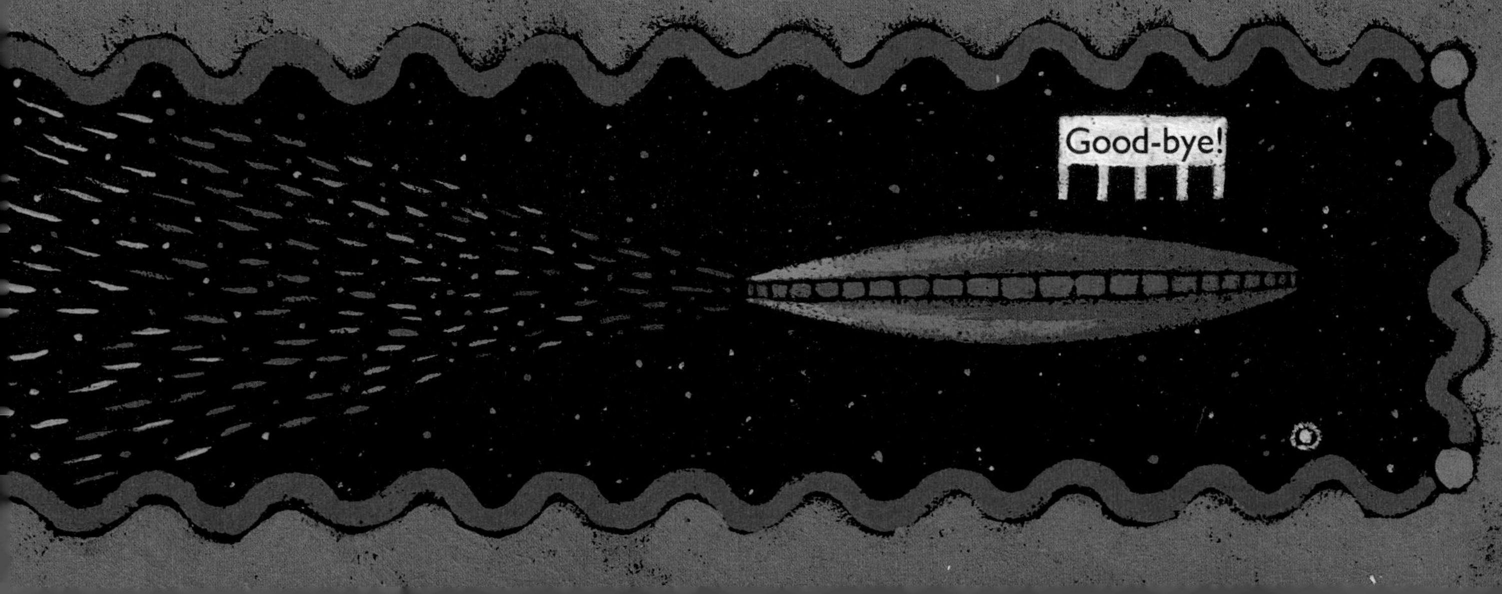
Good-bye!

OUR TRIP TO EARTH

THE GREAT WALL OF CHINA IN ASIA

THE PYRAMIDS IN AFRICA

REDWOOD FOREST IN NORTH AMERICA

INCAN RUINS IN SOUTH AMERICA

SNOW SCULPTURE IN ANTARCTICA

SKIING IN THE ALPS IN EUROPE

THE GREAT BARRIER REEF IN AUSTRALIA

THE EARTH - A BEAUTIFUL PLANET!